Write On

Is Lion Sick?

Gina Nuttall

QED Publishing

First published in the UK in 2005 by
QED Publishing
A Quarto Group company
226 City Road
London EC1V 2TT
www.qed-publishing.co.uk

A Catalogue record for this book is available from the British Library.

ISBN 1 84538 180 7

Written by Gina Nuttall
Designed by Alix Wood
Editor Hannah Ray
Photographer Michael Wicks
Costumes made by Melanie Grimshaw

Series Consultant Anne Faundez
Publisher Steve Evans
Creative Director Louise Morley
Editorial Manager Jean Coppendale

With thanks to Danielle, Ricky,
Lakia, Billy, Jack and Poppy

Printed and bound in China

Cast list

Narrator

Lion

Fox

Cow

Rabbit

Duck

Props

- A mask and a set of cardboard animal footprints for each animal character
- A blanket
- A metal stand or rail, some curtain rings and a length of material for the curtain
- A sign saying 'Lion's Den'
- A stool and a copy of this book (for the narrator)

Setting

The play takes place in and around Lion's den. At the start of the play, only Lion and the narrator are on stage. Lion is pacing about outside his den. Across the entrance to Lion's den is a curtain, which is pulled back. Inside the den we can see Lion's blanket on the floor.

Narrator: It was a very hot day. Lion was hungry, but he was too lazy to look for food.

Lion: Goodness me! I'm really, REALLY hungry, but it's so hot. I can't be bothered to go and look for my dinner. What shall I do? (*Sits down.*)

Narrator: Lion sat down to think. He frowned and scratched his head.

Lion: (*Jumping up*) I know! My dinner can come and look for me! I will pretend to be sick.

Narrator: So Lion went into his den and climbed into bed.

(*Lion gets into bed and draws the curtain across the den entrance.*)

Lion's Den

Narrator:	News of Lion's illness began to reach the other animals. (*Cow enters, followed by Rabbit.*)
Cow:	Rabbit, come here. I have something to tell you. Have you heard about Lion? He's in bed. He is sick.
Rabbit:	Oh no, poor Lion. (*Waves for Duck to enter.*) Duck, come here. (*Duck enters.*) I have something to tell you. Lion is in bed. He is very sick.
Duck:	Oh dear, poor Lion! (*Motions for Fox to enter.*) Fox, come here. (*Fox enters.*) I have something to tell you. Lion is in bed. He is very, VERY sick.
Fox:	(*Scratching his chin*) Oh, is he now? Hmmm! That's very, VERY interesting.

7

Narrator:	The animals discussed what to do.
Cow:	I do feel sorry for Lion.
Rabbit:	Me too. It's no fun being sick.
Duck:	I have an idea! Let's go and visit him.
Cow:	That's a good idea. I will sing a song for him.
Rabbit:	And I will do a dance for him.
Duck:	And I will tell him a very funny joke.
Fox:	Hmmm! This is strange. Lion looked fine when I saw him yesterday. (*Shaking his finger*) I'm warning you. Be very careful. Lion can't be trusted.

(*Cow, Duck, Rabbit and Fox exit.*) |

Narrator:	In spite of Fox's warning, Cow decided to visit Lion.
	(*Cow enters and walks towards Lion's den, laying footprints as she goes.*)
Cow:	I'm a brave cow. I'm not afraid of Lion – especially not of a sick Lion.
	(*Cow mimes knocking on the curtain.*)
Narrator:	Knock, knock.
Lion:	(*Weakly*) Who is it?
Cow:	It's me, Cow. I've come to visit you. I have a song to sing to you.
Lion:	How kind of you! Come in, my friend.
	(*Cow disappears behind the curtain.*)
Narrator:	So Cow went in. But did any of you see her come out?
	(*Curtain shakes. Cow's mask is thrown out from behind it.*)

Lion's
Den

11

Narrator:	The next day, Rabbit followed Cow's footprints to Lion's den. *(Rabbit enters and walks towards Lion's den, laying footprints as he goes.)*
Rabbit:	I'm a brave rabbit. I'm not afraid of Lion – especially not of a sick Lion. *(Rabbit mimes knocking on the curtain.)*
Narrator:	Knock, knock.
Lion:	*(Weakly)* Who is it?
Rabbit:	It's me, Rabbit. I've come to visit you. I have a dance to do for you.
Lion:	How kind of you! Come in, my friend. *(Rabbit disappears behind the curtain.)*
Narrator:	So Rabbit went in. But did any of you see him leave? *(Curtain shakes. Rabbit's mask is thrown out from behind it.)*

Narrator:	The next day, Duck followed Cow and Rabbit's footprints to Lion's den.
	(Duck enters and walks towards Lion's den, laying footprints as she goes.)
Duck:	I'm a brave duck. I'm not afraid of Lion – especially not of a sick Lion.
	(Duck mimes knocking on the curtain.)
Narrator:	Knock, knock.
Lion:	*(Weakly)* Who is it?
Duck:	It's me, Duck. I've come to visit you. I have a very funny joke for you.
Lion:	How kind of you! Come in, my friend.
	(Duck disappears behind the curtain.)
Narrator:	So Duck went in. But did any of you see her go home?
	(Curtain shakes. Duck's mask is thrown out from behind it.)

Narrator:	Finally, it was Fox's turn. He followed Cow and Rabbit and Duck's footprints to Lion's den.
	(Fox enters and walks towards Lion's den, laying footprints as he goes.)
Fox:	*(To the audience)* I'm not a brave fox. But I am clever. Watch!
	(Fox mimes knocking on the curtain.)
Narrator:	Knock, knock.
Lion:	*(Weakly)* Who is it?
Fox:	It's me, Fox. I heard that you were sick. Tell me, Lion, how are you now?
Lion:	Oh, not very well, my friend. But do come in! I'm sure I will feel much better for seeing you.

Fox:	And I'm sure that I will feel much better for NOT seeing you! I can see all these footprints going into your den, but none coming out. You tricked Cow, Rabbit and Duck into visiting you, and then you gobbled them up for your dinner. Goodbye, Lion!

(Fox strides off stage, leaving a trail of footprints. Lion pokes his head out from behind the curtain.)

Lion:	Oh bother! Fox has found me out.
Narrator:	So Lion had no dinner that day. Clever old Fox saw to that!

18

Lion's
Den

19

What do you think?

How many characters are there in this play? Can you name them all?

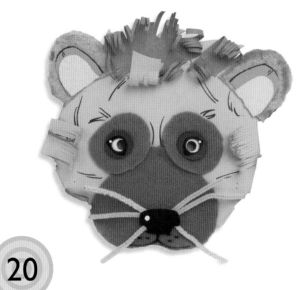

Go on a word hunt. How many times can you find the word 'Lion'?

Why didn't Lion go
and look for food?

Lion's
Den

What were Cow,
Rabbit and Duck
each going to do
for Lion when
they went to visit?

What do you think might have happened if Fox had gone in to see Lion?

Did you feel sorry for Lion at the end of the play? Why?

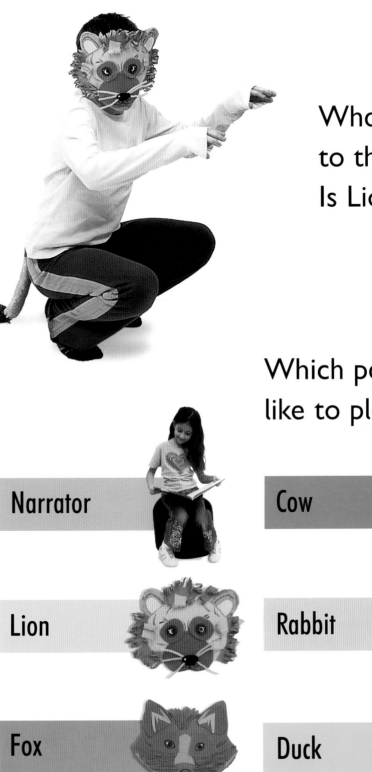

What is the answer
to the question:
Is Lion sick?

Which part would you
like to play? Why?

Narrator

Cow

Lion

Rabbit

Fox

Duck

23

Parents' and teachers' notes

- Ask your child to recall the events of the play in sequence. Prompt with questions such as, 'What happened at the beginning of the play?' 'What happened next?' 'What happened at the end?' Encourage your child to pick out the most significant events.

- Ask your child what Lion was thinking as he sat down on pages 4–5. Draw the outline of a thought bubble and help your child to write Lion's thought in it.

- Ask your child to draw a picture of a scene from the play. Help him or her to write one or two sentences to describe it.

- Together, think of five words to describe Lion. Your child could draw a picture of Lion and write the five words around the picture.

- Ask your child to imagine that the play 'Is Lion Sick?' is coming to a theatre near you, and to make a poster to advertise it.

- Look at page 10 and find the sentence, 'Who is it?' Ask your child what kind of sentence it is (a question). How can he or she tell it is a question? Can they find any other questions in the play?

- Discuss with your child how he or she can tell this is a play. Point out the different type, and explain this is called *italic* print. Explain that the words in *italics* tell the actors what to do, and are not to be spoken aloud.

- Explain to your child that this play is based on a fable, which is a traditional story that teaches a lesson. The lesson is called the 'moral' of the story. Ask your child what he or she thinks the moral of this story is. (Learn from others' mistakes.)

- Talk with your child about the role of the narrator. Explain that the narrator helps to tell the story, filling in detail that is not in the characters' speeches.

- Encourage your child to act out the play with friends or family members. Alternatively, he or she could make finger puppets and present the play as a puppet show.

- Find other versions of this fable, or other Aesop fables, and read them with your child. Compare the different versions. What is the moral of each story?

- Talk to your child about any play he or she might have seen. Was it a stage play like this one, with people playing the parts, or was it a puppet show where people say the words but work puppets to act out the story? Was there a narrator? What did your child like about the play?

- Look at the photographs of the children performing the play. Discuss how the costumes identify each character. Does your child have a favourite character? Together, make a costume for your child.